REDUX

TRANSFIGURATION

A
Divine
Encounter
&
Conversation:
Moses, Jesus & Elijah

J.R.R. JAQUEZ

ISBN: 9798992224030

DEDICATION

To my mother, Marisela, who in many ways believed in the supernatural.
And, as a medical doctor, she showed commiseration and compassion for others in many ways. Somewhere in the Promised Land, a divine encounter and conversation with you.

January 17, 1951 - August 31, 2023

Prologue

With a Judeo-Christian tradition as its backdrop, this story explores and expands upon a supernatural event—the Transfiguration. The focus tilts toward the Christian tradition while maintaining elements of the Jewish heritage.

At the heart of this narrative is not the lives of the protagonists themselves but the event that unites them. In Spanish, one might say the event "protagoniza"—it takes center stage

Drawing from the Gospel accounts in Matthew 17: 1-13, Mark 9:2-13, and Luke 9:28-36, this story blends elements from all three to create a cohesive and chronological sequence. While faithful to these texts, the narrative takes creative liberties to make the story accessible and engaging, which avoids potential confusion or tedium from disjointed accounts.

Embedded within modern details and expressions, balanced with respect for the sacredness of the event. The author employs poetic and theological licenses to expand upon the profound conversation that the Gospels reference but do not elaborate on. Together, let us explore this divine encounter.

INTRODUCTION

In Redux Transfiguration, the story's backdrop is a supernatural event within the Judeo-Christian tradition. Readers familiar with figures such as Jesus, Moses, Peter, James, John, and Elijah will find their appreciation enriched by prior knowledge of these characters. For those with backgrounds in theology, religious studies, or similar fields, the narrative offers an additional layer of depth.

However, familiarity with these traditions is not a prerequisite. The story is crafted to be accessible to a broader audience, including those interested in theology, spiritual literature, or Christian-themed fiction. While such readers may experience the story differently, its essence remains engaging and thought-provoking.

The tone, rhythm, and pacing mirror the Gospels. This is not a conventional protagonist-versus-antagonist story; rather, it is contemplative in nature. While some conflict exists, the narrative focuses on the profound themes of faith, identity, and destiny; the narrative follows the tone of Matthew 17:1-13, Mark 9:2-13, and Luke 9:28-36.

To preserve the story's flow, additional insights, clarifications, or theological notes will be provided after the narrative. This avoids disrupting the reader's immersion. Let us now ascend toward Tabor and witness the unfolding of a divine mystery.

CHAPTER I
THE ASCENT OF TABOR

Like foaming waves of the sea, clouds in linen strands embrace the mustard-yellow sun… submerging it beneath the turquoise sky.

As the sun sinks… clouds knit a cashmere cascade, cradling the moon. The current shepherds the sphere upwards toward the sapphire horizon… dressing it in bone white, letting it float.

An orange dew stains the cheeks and chin of the clouds.

West of the Sea of Galilee and East of Nazareth, the Rabbi marches toward the mountain. Six days ago, a dream stirred his soul. He leads a triangular procession: Peter to his right, John behind him, and James to his left.

Footprints mark their climb, dust clinging to their sandals as the heat presses on them. Shadows offer fleeting relief as they wipe sweat from their brows. Once at the mountain's foot, Jesus and his disciples pause to take in the surroundings.

They stand side by side; their eyes trace the mountain's features: its base, valley, plateau, slope, crest, ridge, canyon, and summit. To broaden their perspective, the travelers spread out. They notice the dome shape and a prominent plateau midway up.

The Rabbi regathers them to discuss a route. He chooses a path crossing the plateau and ridge, where he will leave them before ascending further on his own. In a serpentine line, Jesus leads, followed by John, James, and Peter. Because the rugged terrain shifts beneath their feet, they extend their hands for balance and support.

As they climb, the Rabbi notices the ridge ahead and calls for a pause. They marvel at the shifting clouds, which seem to dance with the sapphire-turquoise skies.

At the ridge, sweat trickles down their brows. A breeze swirls around them, whispering, "Look up." They obey. Their eyes widen in unison as smiles pass among them. The vast expanse above greets each one, and they contemplate the sky's endless blue hues; it invites them to pause and rest.

The Rabbi surveys the summit. After a moment of silent contemplation, he meets each disciple's eyes, one by one. With his right index finger, he points toward the summit and outlines his plan to reach it. Peter interrupts, worry etched into his voice: "Rabbi, be careful."

With serene confidence, the Rabbi lowers his head in a gesture of affirmation. "Wait here. I'll return after I pray." Lowering his arm, he journeys toward the summit. As he leaves, Peter frowns; worry deepens the lines on his face Within minutes, the disciples lose sight of him. Drawn to fulfill a vision stirring within, the Rabbi journeys forth alone—following the silent call of fate and prayer.

CHAPTER II
PRECIPITOUS PETER

Peter, James, and John look up at the summit; heads raised to get a better view. Eagerness engulfs them in anticipation of the Rabbi's arrival.

Peter, whispering to himself, fixes his eyes on the steep ascent:
"That climb looks so treacherous…"

His brow furrows. He crosses his arms, then taps his foot with the speed of a hummingbird's wings. His heart races, his blood pressure rises, and his face flushes guava red. Shallow breaths follow as urgency swells within him. Then, like a lightning bolt, he bolts from the ridge, following the Rabbi's path.

James and John exchange confused glances as Peter's silhouette dissolves into the distance. James feels a knot in his stomach; a pinch of concern spreads through his chest.

James, frowning and muttering:
"Where is he going?
The Rabbi told us to 'Wait here.'"

Shaking his head, he turns to John, leans close, and whispers: 'Wait here.'

Without waiting for a response, James dashes after Peter.

John stands alone, perplexed. Their disobedience unsettles him. Turning in a full circle, he searches for some explanation but finds none. Suddenly, silence succumbs with the sharp screech of an eagle that draws his gaze toward the sky.

Circling three times, the eagle hovers above him. Its wings shimmering with the hues of Tekhelet, golden streaks tracing the edges. On the third pass, it flies so close their eyes meet—a connection that seems to mark him with a purpose yet to be fulfilled. A shiver runs through John's spine. As the eagle ascends and disappears into the heavens, solitude creeps over him like an unwelcome fog.

Meanwhile, James closes the gap between himself and Peter. His footsteps echo against the rugged terrain. With an outstretched hand, he reaches for the hem of Peter's himation, brushing it before grasping it with firmness.

James pulls Peter to a halt; he spins him around to face him. His left index finger sinks into Peter's chest as he locks eyes with him.

James, sternly:

"Peter, the Rabbi told us to stay.

You can't just run off like this!"

Peter stammers, his voice trembling, raising

his hands defensively:

"He has taken too long!

What if he needs us?"

James exhales sharply, raising an eyebrow.

With his right hand, he points back toward

the ridge:

"No. He hasn't taken too long.

We should go back and wait."

Peter, insistent, his shoulders rigid, shakes

his head:

"James, I'm telling you.

He might be in trouble!"

While the two argue, John, now overcome with concern for his friends, decides to trail them. Solitude gnaws at his resolve, and doubt clouds his thoughts. Recalling the path James took, he walks James' Way for about two miles before spotting them in the distance.

Approaching cautiously, John joins their conversation, placing a calming hand on Peter's shoulder.

John, gently:

"Peter, I understand your worry, but James is right. The Rabbi gave clear instructions. He told us to wait."

Peter's shoulders relax as John's gentle tone trespasses his worry. He exhales, his gaze softens as his head rises and falls. With some coaxing, the two reassure Peter, melting his fears like wax dripping from a candle. Finally, Peter sighs and and tilts his head in assent. Taking James' Way toward the ridge, the trio begins their trek in a straight line.

As they reach the ridge, their worry fades and awe thrives. From the ridge, they see him—his figure bathed in the ethereal glow of a mustard-yellow sun and a bone-white moon—both human and divine. Relief washes over them as the mountain air seems lighter. Exhaling deeply, Peter places a hand over his heart while James and John exchange knowing glances, their spirits lifted by the sight.

CHAPTER III
THE DIVINE ENCOUNTER

The Rabbi reaches the triangular, dome-shaped summit. Dust clings to his tunic, a reminder of an earlier misstep. A bruise mars his left forearm, but he presses on undeterred.

Captivated by the panoramic view, he pauses to catch his breath, Counterclockwise, his gaze sweeps across the land, from the northern hills to the southern valleys, from the eastern horizon to the western plains. The vast splendor mesmerizes him.

For eighteen minutes, he stands immersed in the beauty of creation. Then, closing his eyes, he inclines his head, raises his hands to eye level, and begins to pray. Silence envelops the summit as the minutes stretch into nearly an hour.

In the heights, above him, the heavens awaken.

Turning like celestial gears, clouds swirl into the shape of an hourglass. On one side, linen clouds spin clockwise; on the other, wool clouds mirror the contrary motion. Together, they weave a shimmering tapestry. It resonates like the beat of a divine dance.

The rhythmic stomps of hidden feet resound in the heavens.

The clouds dance to the tune of the Hora; the Hora weaves thin Tekhelet curtains that cascade before him. The rocks tremble as the swirling navels, resembling the eyes of a cyclone, start to open...

The tremor ripples through the mountain, its vibrations like the heartbeat that connects summit to ridge. The disciples felt the faint hum, its rhythm rising from the summit like the pulse of the mountain itself. Startled, they glance upward, drawn to the source.

The Hora stirs them to their feet. Capturing the revelation like the aperture of a camera, their eyes widen and mouths hang open.

James murmurs, his voice tinged with awe:
"He commands the winds and clouds.
What sort of man is this?"

As the swirling navels open at the center of the two bulbs, two luminous figures emerge from each navel. Wrapped in Lightning-Umbilical Cords that coil around their waists like living vines, they descend with measured grace. Cradled by cascading Tekhelet curtains and accompanied by a gentle, cool breeze, they reach the summit.

One figure lands to the Rabbi's right, the other to his left. Their radiant forms cast a blue light that shifts and dances across the Rabbi's tunic. As if absorbing their presence into his soul, he stands still for a moment. The cords uncoil and ascend back to the heavens, as the celestial dance subsides.

Enchanted by the two luminous figures, the disciples gaze upward. Their expressions mirror Edvard Munch's *The Scream*—but inverted: wide with wonder, mouths agape, hands motionless. Let's call it *The Awe*. Trying to grasp the impossibility of what he's witnessing, James raises a hand to his cheek. Casting a sublime glow over the mountain, both sun and moon conspire to shine together. Time seems to bend.

Since their arrival, the two men contemplate Jesus and his immediate surroundings. The man to Jesus' left wears a leather belt around his waist and a cloak that covers his luminous head down to his eyebrows. The man to Jesus' right dons a veil down to his shoulders; it conceals his radiant face down to his eyebrows.

Minutes later, the clouds begin to disappear... The Rabbi lowers his hands, raises his head, and opens his eyes. His gaze ascends, pauses heavenward, then gently lowers. The receding clouds leave the summit shrouded in stillness, broken only by the faint rustle of the breeze. For seven heavenly minutes, no words are spoken. Finally, he smiles, the stillness evaporates with a greeting:

"Shalom Aleichem."

The veiled figure responds:
"Aleichem Shalom."

The cloaked man inclines his head and echoes:
"Shalom Aleichem."

For a moment, the only sound is the faint hum of the retreating clouds. The Rabbi, the veiled man, and the cloaked man stand united as one—earth, prophecy, and heaven, bound in an eternal stillness.

CHAPTER IV
THE DIVINE CONVERSATION

Casting a gentle glow over the summit, a shimmering halo encircles the clouds above.

From the heavens, a celestial voice resonates:

"This is my Son, whom I love.

With Him, I am well pleased.

He is the Chosen One...

Listen to Him!"

Reaching every ear, the words reverberate through the mountain. On the ridge, Peter, James, and John fall to their knees. A mustard-yellow halo radiates from the Rabbi's face, edged with tips reminiscent of Palm Sunday fronds. His tunic gleams in the same golden hue.

The veiled man steps forward, his voice calm yet weighty:

"Shalom Aleichem. Chosen One."

Inclining his head, the cloaked man echoes:

"Shalom Aleichem. Son of God."

Surveying the vast land below, both adjust to the summit's height. Like camels that travel step by step in the desert, they move with patience and cover only a few feet each minute or two. The veiled man's gaze shifts between the landscape and the Chosen One. Vigilant as a sand fox, the cloaked man observes the Son of

God and the three distant figures on the ridge. Silent, the Rabbi absorbs their intent.

The veiled man's gaze lingers on the terrain. The land's essence resonates within him. A flicker of déjà vu crosses his radiant face, he pauses. Tilting his head slightly, he presses two fingers to his lips in contemplation. Slowly, he steps toward the Rabbi.

When he is within arm's reach, he narrows his eyes and asks:
"Is this the land beyond the Jordan River?
The land that flows with milk and honey?"

A fluvial voice flows within him, an unexpected delight.

The Chosen One's lips curl into a gentle smile:

"Yes. This is the land beyond the Jordan.

The Promised Land."

The veiled man's eyes widen. As if to feel its promise, he kneels placing two fingers on the soil. For a moment, he is still, absorbing its warmth.

His eyes misted with longing:

"To see this land after so long... it feels like a gift."

Rising, he returns to his place and speaks with a somber tone:

"I begged Yahweh to let me enter this land, but He denied me. I made a mistake—a grave one. I was tired, angry. He told me to speak to the rock, but I struck it once... Waited and

nothing... Then again! I lost myself in

frustration, called the people rebels, and took

credit for what was His.

The water was Yahweh's gift—not mine to give."

The Rabbi nods, his gaze unwavering:

"You always used the rod to demonstrate

Yahweh's power.

Why speak to the rock this time?

What changed?"

The veiled man sighs deeply, his voice carrying

the weight of regret:

"Valid questions. What changed, indeed?

Who changed Yahweh's heart?"

The Rabbi's voice softens:

"I asked Yahweh to let you see this land

—the Promised Land.

Then, I dreamed of this summit, and it became

the way."

The veiled man tilts his head while flames of

curiosity flicker in his gaze:

"The Son asks the Father. Why?"

The Rabbi responds with conviction:

"Because of your effort, endurance, leadership,

and commitment.

You have done so much for us."

The veiled man inclines his head, curiosity

softening his voice:

"Your mother—did she ever ask you for something?"

Recalling a cherished memory with quiet fondness, the Rabbi's gaze softened; his expression lightens…

He began:

"Yes. At a wedding in Cana. The wine had run out, and she quietly came to me, saying, 'They have no more wine.'"

The veiled man lifts an eyebrow:

"And what did you do?"

The Rabbi hesitates, his gaze distant:

"At first, I resisted. I told her it wasn't my time. But she simply turned to the servants and said, 'Do whatever he tells you.'"

The cloaked man chuckles softly, his tone edged with humor. A faint smile tugs his lips:
"So… she gave you no choice."

The Rabbi smiles and nods, admiration glinting in his eyes:
"She trusted me completely. First, I told the servants to fill six stone jars with water. Then, I instructed them to draw some out for the master of the banquet."

The veiled man crosses his arms, tilting his head in disbelief:
"Wait, I'm confused… You told the servants to give water to the master? So he could taste it!?"

The Rabbi chuckles softly:
"Oh. By then, it was wine. And guess what?

He called the bridegroom aside and said, 'You have saved the best wine for last.'"

The veiled man gazes skyward, his expression one of wonder:
"Each jar held twenty to thirty gallons.
You turned over one hundred gallons of water into wine? The best wine?"

The Rabbi nods.
"My mother's compassion saw a need, and her faith moved me to act. I understood."

The veiled man smiles, his voice softening:
"What is her name?"

The Rabbi replies, his tone reverent:
"Mari. Her name is Mary."

The veiled man steps back, his voice filled with quiet admiration:
"The Mother asks the Son, and the Son asks the Father. What a profound grace!"

The veiled man and The Chosen exchange glances. They understand each other.

The veiled man:
"Besides you and your mother, anyone else at the wedding?"

The Chosen One pauses, in thought:
"Yes."

With an open hand, he lifts it, pointing straight toward the horizon:
"Walk over there. Look down."

As the veiled man walks to the edge, the cloaked man glances down at the disciples, then at the Son of God. Pointing with his right index finger, he asks:

"Who are they?
Are those the ones who attended the wedding?"

The Son of God:
"Yes. They are my disciples."

The cloaked man:
"So, are all of them bound to you in a special way?
Does a profound sense of loyalty dwell within them toward you?"

The Son of God nods:
"Yes. Between us, that is true."

The cloaked man's voice turns grave:
"One will deny you."

The Son of God, surprised:
"Deny me? Who? When?"

The cloaked man hesitates, then shakes his head:
"'When?' I see guards... change of guards...
'Who?'
Their destinies intertwine. In due time... You will see."

He raises his right arm and looks directly:
"I see your exodus in Jerusalem.
Are you aware of what awaits...?
The sacrifice...?"

With a somber tone, the Son of God replies:
"Yes. I know. I know."

The cloaked man steps forward, his voice heavy with memory. He frowns and lowers one arm then places his other hand on his chest; it mirrors El Greco's *"The Nobleman with his Hand on his Chest."*

The cloaked man:
"Once, despair dragged me into an abyss so deep I begged Yahweh to take my life.
But what I felt—what broke me—will be nothing compared to the agony you will endure."

The cloaked man pauses, gazing downward. Before he continues, the veiled man steps closer and interjects:

"I, too, once felt the same way.

I asked Yahweh to end my life.

But Yahweh helped me.

Seventy elders helped me.

What happened to you? Any help?"

The cloaked man's voice lowers:

"Fearing for my life, I fled. Exhausted, I thought

it was the end... An angel woke me and offered

bread, warm and fresh, and water. I ate and

drank, and Yahweh restored me. I didn't know

strength could taste so simple. "

The veiled man lowers and raises his head

slowly:

"Even in despair, Yahweh provides.

Let us fulfill the divine purpose together."

The cloaked man nods:

"Together? Yes."

The veiled man fluctuates his sight between The Chosen One, the men below and the cloaked man.

He pauses and focuses on the cloaked man:

"Yes, one of them will deny him."

Then, the veiled man turns to the Chosen One:

"One will falter, but another will stand by you. In time, you'll understand."

The veiled man pauses.

Then, he walks towards The Chosen One and stops midway:

"A political ambush awaits you.

You will face a monarch.

I faced one.

Speak your truth.

The weight of salvation rests on your shoulders,

Chosen One."

The cloaked man's voice lowers, trembling with

foreknowledge:

"Blood…

In a garden, you will sweat blood.

Your shoulders, back, brow and side will bleed.

Through it, salvation will flow"

The Son of God inclines his head. The
participants remain still. Silence intoxicates the
air for about 40 seconds. Then, a vision flashes

within the veiled man, so he turns and walks toward the edge.

The veiled man observes the disciples:
"The eagle unfolded its wings and crosses the skies.
The message endures; the teachings survive."

Immediately after, the veiled man approaches the cloaked man. He whispers in his ear, and the cloaked man listens and murmurs. After about three minutes, the cloaked man nods. They turn and start to walk toward The Chosen One, The Son of God.

The veiled man stands at the Rabbi's right shoulder, and the cloaked man stays on the left. Once in place, the veiled man raises his hands, interlaces his middle, index, and ring fingers against the veil, and pulls it back to reveal his face and head. The cloaked man mirrors his companion's movements. As if they carried the weight of ages past, their radiant expressions reflected a profound understanding.

The veiled man speaks, his voice steady yet solemn:
"You changed the water into wine, and through Your actions, You moved Yahweh's heart, granting me this moment to see the Promised Land.
Thank you for showing me this land.
I, we, wish to lay our hands upon you."

Three heartbeats pass in stillness. Turning right, the Rabbi raises his head. His eyes meet those of the unveiled man. Across the expanse of time, they connect. An infinitesimal but eternal smile graces the Rabbi's lips. Turning left, he meets the uncloaked man's gaze. A silent river of understanding flows between them... No words are spoken.

Positioning themselves diametrically on the Rabbi's left and right, the two form a perfect symmetry, with the Rabbi standing central in their alignment.

The unveiled man makes a petition to the Chosen One that includes two names. The uncloaked man overhears and makes the same petition, but with one name. The Rabbi gazes sideways and nods as he grants their requests.

The unveiled man places one hand on the Rabbi's shoulder and the other on his head.

The uncloaked man mirrors him, their movements forming a perfect symmetry. Then, the Rabbi raises his hands to waist level, palms up.

A warm breeze ripples across the summit, threading through their hair and robes like an unseen hymn. The Rabbi begins to speak, his voice imbued with a resonance that seems to echo through time. In a rhythm only he knows, his voice rises and falls. The other two join him. In perfect harmony, their voices blend. His tunic glows brighter. Cloven tongues of fire flicker above their heads with a brilliance greater than the Morning Star; the glow illuminates the summit.

The clouds start to turn; their hum deepens, reverberating through the mountain.

In the skies, a gradual sound of hand claps and foot stomps grows. Above, the clouds swirl to the rhythm of the Debka. Spinning counter to one another, two Tekhelet rings take shape. From their radiant centers, twin staircases shimmered with light unfurl—each bordered by a Lightning-Umbilical Handrail. Their ascent form a bridge between heaven and earth, between the mortal and the divine.

At the ridge, the disciples shield their eyes, barely able to glimpse the radiant figures at the summit. The light pulsed with a living brilliance, its radiance sears into their souls and leaves them overwhelmed and awestruck. Tabor trembles under their feet. Unable to bear the radiance and overcome by awe, their eyes close, knees buckle, and they fall prostrate, their faces pressed into the earth.

CHAPTER V
THE DESCENT OF TABOR

The air is still, and the mountain seems to hum with divine energy. Below the summit and immersed in the afterglow from it, the Rebbe stands on the ridge before his disciples. Lying flat with their hands over their heads and faces pressed into the soil, they tremble.

The Rabbi:

"Get up... Do not be afraid..."

Peter raises his head and glances sideways. He kneels, and his eyes peer past the Rabbi's shoulders toward the summit.

There, two spiral stairways stretch toward the heavens—one made of Tekhelet-linen clouds, the other of Tekhelet-wool clouds. Their shapes resemble the snow-white stairways inside La Sagrada Familia's cathedral, rising toward the Rabbi's right and left shoulders, as if the heavens were opening to meet them.

Peter leaps to his feet, his arms wide with excitement:
"Rabbi! This place—this is good! Should we stay here?
I could build three shelters—one for you, one for..."

He falters, his eyes scanning the summit.

His voice lowers, tinged with confusion:

"...Who are they?"

The Rabbi turns slowly, his gaze calm and unwavering. He speaks quietly, as if the answer has always been known:

"Moses. Elijah."

Peter's eyes widen, his excitement mixing with awe:

"Moses and Elijah... here?"

The Rabbi nods, his expression serene:

"Yes."

John and James lift their heads at Peter's words, their curiosity piqued. James turns to John, his voice low and tentative:

"The summit... the Rabbi... he stood there with them.

How is this possible?"

John interrupts, his tone urgent:
"Forget that! Look at the summit!"

James follows John's gaze, his eyes widening. Two stairways of clouds rise straight into the heavens, their geometric shapes—one heptagonal, the other rhomboid. Connecting earth and sky, a Lightning-Umbilical Handrail coils around each stairway.

James murmurs:

"Moses climbs one. Elijah the other."

James and John kneel. John stands. He brushes the dust from his clothes. After almost two minutes, he notices that James stays motionless, eyes wide like soup bowls, so he reaches and grabs James' right underarm. He lifts him. They overheard the dialogue between the Rabbi and Peter, so they join the conversation.

John:

"Rabbi, how do you know their names? You asked? They said it?"

Rabbi:

"Their stories and anointing revealed their identities."

James, still awestruck:

"This transformative, heaven-on-earth experience!

I cannot wait to share it with the others!"

The Rabbi's expression turns firm.

"No. You cannot tell anyone. That goes for all of you."

Peter, incredulous, gestures wildly toward the summit:

"What? No one? But why? Look at this!

How can we not share it with others?"

John adds:

"Yes! I agree with James and Peter.

And, what did you speak of?

Did they speak of us?"

Rebbe:

"... Now, is not the time.

The time will come...

Time to go..."

The leader guides them down the mountain; he passes between them. For a few moments, they contemplate Moses and Elijah; both ascend the stairways to heaven. Then, Peter and James march behind Jesus: Peter to his right and James to his left.

John takes one last look at each ladder. He gazes at it from its base at the mountain's summit to its peak in the sky. When his gaze reaches the peak, he sees what appear to be distant, blurry starlights. Two lights descend Moses' ladder, and one descends Elijah's. However, he refocuses and quickens his pace to catch up with the others, letting the vision fade.

By now, the moonlight floods the landscape, softening the path ahead. Pockets of mustard sunlight linger in the distance, a reminder of the summit's splendor. The Rabbi guides them along a different route. Curiosity bites at Peter as he leans toward the Rabbi's right ear.

Peter:

"Rabbi, on the way to the summit…

any troubles… ?"

The Rabbi lifts his left forearm, revealing the

faint bruise:

"I slipped and left a mark."

Peter gasps, turning to James:

"You see! I knew he was in trouble!"

James shakes his head in disbelief and lifts

the left arm, exasperated:

"You dashed off like lightning!

How about a heads-up next time?"

Peter chuckles, raising his hands defensively:

"Perhaps. Still, I was right to worry!"

The Rabbi listens to their banter with a small smile. Meanwhile, stealing a glance over his shoulder, John slows his pace. In the distance, three luminous figures descend the stairways. He hesitates but eventually quickens his steps to rejoin the group.

Concealing the summit from view, the path curves. As they trace it down, the Rabbi senses an absence.

Turning, he calls:

"John... ?"

He steps back then moves between Peter and James:

"Wait here... Both..."

Walking about one and half a mile, the Rabbi traces the curve, and finds John mesmerized; he gazes at each staircase.

In the middle of heaven and earth, John sees three luminous figures standing in Moses' stairway and two in Elijah's. While holding the Lightning-Umbilical Handrail and enveloped in a divine glow, the figures contemplate the Promised Land. Approaching quietly, the teacher stops beside him.

Rebbe:

"What do you see?"

John, startled:

"Rebbe... hi.

So, Rebbe... I see three figures in one

stairway and two in the other.."

Rebbe moves his head up and down:

"Yes... Time to go, John."

The Rabbi walks down, and John begins

to walk in his footsteps but pauses, a

question lingering on his lips:

"Rebbe, is it Moses and Elijah with others?

Or is it someone else? Do you know who

they are?"

The Rabbi sighs, meeting John's gaze:

"Yes. Moses and Elijah.

Moses with his brother Aaron and sister

Miriam.

Elijah's pupil, Elisha, who was like a son to

him."

John:

"They stand together... as one?"

Rebbe lowers his chin:

"In a familial way..."

After a pause, the Rebbe's tone turns
serious, his gaze steady:
"Remember, John.
You cannot tell anyone what you have
witnessed."

John places a hand on his chest:
"Do not worry, Rabbi. I will not."

The Rabbi incline his head and motions
toward the path:
"Let us go, John.
Tormented souls in need of liberation await
us; we must heal them."

John smiles; Rebbe smiles. Side by side, they walk to meet and regroup with the others. Once more and touched by the echoes of heaven, he leads them down to the valley: Peter to his right, John behind him, and James to his left. The valley below seemed both familiar and transformed as it came into view.

In silence, they walk. Under the mantle of the Prince of Peace, they walk. A sea of tranquility submerges them, its touch soft as fine linen. Exchanging knowing smiles, Peter, James, and John feel the peace that surpasses all understanding—the peace of God.

Epilogue

The summit was left behind, its radiance fading into the twilight as the Rabbi and his disciples descended toward the valley. The disciples accompanied him in silence, their hearts heavy yet strangely at peace. They carried no words for what they had seen— only awe and wonder, etched into their souls like the grooves of a well-worn path.

Peter, James, and John stayed close to the Rabbi, their feet treading the dust of the road. Though their journey would stretch across many days and places, the memory of Tabor would remain with them forever—a moment when time and eternity brushed against one another.

From the ridge, the disciples glimpsed Moses and Elijah—not in flesh and blood as humans might expect, but spiritually present, their radiance transcending the boundaries of earthly existence. For some, this encounter raises profound questions: could Mount Tabor, at just under 1,900 feet in elevation, modest by geographical standards and barely meeting the criteria for a mountain, truly hold such divine significance? In biblical narratives, after all, "high mountains" could often mean hills. Now, Tabor's power emanates from its location, which is about 11 miles (18 kilometers) west of the Jordan River.

From its vantage point in Israel, Mount Tabor opens a perspective that bridges the temporal and eternal. Perhaps Moses, who had gazed upon the Promised Land long ago, now saw it fully—not with human eyes, but with spiritual ones. The Rabbi had moved Yahweh's heart, so this action grants Moses this moment.

The disciples, too, wrestled with what they had witnessed. Was the exchange they observed truly a conversation, or something beyond human comprehension? It felt less like spoken words and more like truths exchanged through divine understanding, transcending the limits of earthly language.

In the quiet of the descent, they knew something had changed. The world below awaited, and the weight of its salvation rested on the shoulders of the One they shadowed.

BIBLICAL CITATIONS

These are the biblical citations that serve as inspiration or sources for each chapter. By "source or inspiration," it means the citation may evoke a particular image, provide content, or sometimes both. One could add other citations but this gives a fair overview and yes a reader might know cultural references or perhaps eastern eggs (Hora, Debka—regional dances). The King James version serves as an overall guide.

Certain citations may appear in more than one chapter, as their imagery or themes continue throughout the narrative. For the overarching context of the entire story, refer to:

- Matthew 17:1-13

- Mark 9:2-13

- Luke 9:28-36

CHAPTER I THE ASCENT OF TABOR

- Exodus 19: gathering with Yahweh—Mount Sinai.

- Matthew 2:13-15, 19-23: travel a destination.

- Luke 24:13-35: The walk to Emmaus.

- 1 Kings 19:12: Elijah's gentle whisper.

CHAPTER II PRECIPITOUS PETER

- Matthew 14:28-31: Peter's impulsiveness onto the water.

- Matthew 26:33-35: Peter's impulsiveness never deny Jesus.

- Galatians 2:11–12: James' authority/leadership.

- Acts 15:13–21: James' authority/leadership.

- Galatians 1:18–19: James' authority/leadership.

- Matthew 4:21-22: agreement between James and John.

- Mark 1:19-20: accord between James and John.

CHAPTER III THE DIVINE ENCOUNTER

- Exodus 19:16: gathering with Yahweh — Mount Sinai

- Luke 8:25: command of natural forces (wind and waves).

- Exodus 34:33-35: the clothing (the veil).

- 2 Kings 1:8: the clothing (leather belt).

- 1 Kings 19:13 clothing (cloak over his head).

CHAPTER IV THE DIVINE CONVERSATION

- Exodus 4:10: fluvial voice.

- Deuteronomy 1:37, 3:23-26, 32:51-52: God denies Moses.

- Numbers 20: 7-11: Moises' disobedience the water.

- Exodus 17: 5-7: hits the rock once Moses.

- Matthew 2:13-15, 19-23: travel a destination.

- John 2:1–11: wedding at Cana.

- Matthew 26:34: Jesus foretells Peter's denial.

- 1 Kings 19: 3-18: helped from an angel.

- Numbers 11:15-17: helped from 70 elders.

- John 19:26-27: entrusts of Jesus' mother.

- Exodus 19: 1-2: monarch/ruler pharaoh.

- John 18: 36-38: monarch/ruler speak your truth.

- Luke 22:44: sweat blood.

- John 19:1-3,18, 34: blood.

- Hebrews 9:22: blood.

- Ephesians 1:7: blood.

- Acts 2:2-4 Tongues of fire.

- John 1: 51: Jacobs ladder reference.

- Genesis 28:10-19: Jacob's dream of the ladder.

CHAPTER V THE DESCENT OF TABOR

- Genesis 28:10-19: Jacob's dream of the ladder.

- Luke 9:37 last response from the Rabbi.

- Philippians 4:7: The peace that transcends all understanding.

ABOUT THE AUTHOR

J.Rodolfo earned a Master of Arts (M.A.) degree from the University of Miami. Over the course of his studies at Miami Dade College, Florida International University and the University of Miami, J.R. pursued coursework in literature (poetry) journalism (print and broadcast), creative writing, theater, and cinema. Over decades, the author has lived a number of spiritual experiences. Furthermore, he has listened to a number of priests, pastors, rabbis and scholars speak, analyze and scrutinized the bible. This background reflects his story. Currently, he resides in South Florida and continues his writing journey.

www.ingramcontent.com/pod-product-compliance
Lightning Source LLC
Chambersburg PA
CBHW020143150626
46552CB00021B/1390